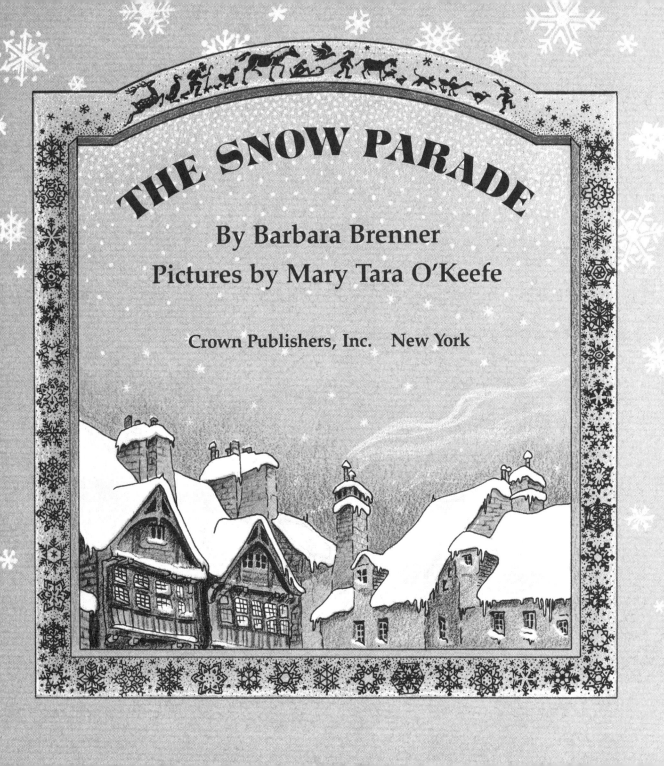

THE SNOW PARADE

By Barbara Brenner
Pictures by Mary Tara O'Keefe

Crown Publishers, Inc.   New York

Library of Congress Cataloging in Publication Data
Brenner, Barbara. The snow parade. Summary: An increasing number of animals
and people join Andrew Barclay in his parade through the snow. [1. Counting.
2. Parades—Fiction. 3. Snow—Fiction] I. O'Keefe, Mary Tara, ill. II. Title.
PZ7.B7518Sn 1984 [E] 83-18999 ISBN 0-517-55210-8

For Tanya   For Tara and Matthew
B.B.   M.T.O'K.

"Who wants to make a snow parade?"
    asked Andrew Barclay.
"I can't," said his sister.
"I won't," said his brother.
"Then I'll make a parade by myself,"
    said Andrew.

So Andrew Barclay went off alone
  to make a parade in the snow.
He marched along in his new red boots.
Marched and marched.
All by himself.
And he was the only *one* in that parade.

Pretty soon he met a spotted dog.
"What are you doing?" the dog asked him.
Andrew answered, "I'm making a parade."
"*One* isn't enough for a parade," said the dog.
"Then you march with me," said Andrew.
"I can't march," said the dog, "but I'll run."

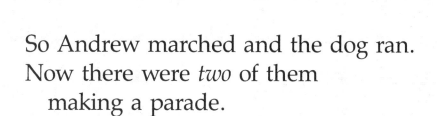

So Andrew marched and the dog ran.
Now there were *two* of them
making a parade.

After a while a duck swam over.
"What are you doing?" asked the duck.
"We're making a parade," said Andrew.
"*Two* is too few for a parade," said the duck.
"I'll swim along with the *two* of you."

So Andrew marched,
　the dog ran,
　and the duck swam.
Now there were *three* of them parading.

A rabbit came by.
"What's this?" asked the rabbit.
Andrew said, "This is a parade."
"I don't call *three* a parade," said the rabbit.
"Then why don't you come along
    and make *four*?"
"I will," said the rabbit.
"I'll hop along in the back."

So Andrew marched,
   the dog ran,
   the duck swam,
   and the rabbit hopped along in the back.
Now there were *four* of them
   making a parade.

A pigeon flew by.
"What's going on down there?"
    called the pigeon.
"A parade," Andrew called back.
  The pigeon said, "It takes more than *four*
      to make a parade."
"Then you come, too," said Andrew.
"Good idea," said the pigeon.
"I'll fly along on the side."

Pigeon flew.
Rabbit hopped.
Duck waddled.
Dog ran.
Andrew marched.
Now there were *five* in the parade.

A policeman rode by on his horse.
"What are you doing?" he asked.
Andrew said, "We're making a parade."
"Oh, no," said the policeman.
"*Five* is a handful but it's not a parade.
We'll have to come along with you."

The policeman rode at the front.
He made *six*.
And his horse made *seven*.
Now there were *seven* in the snow parade.

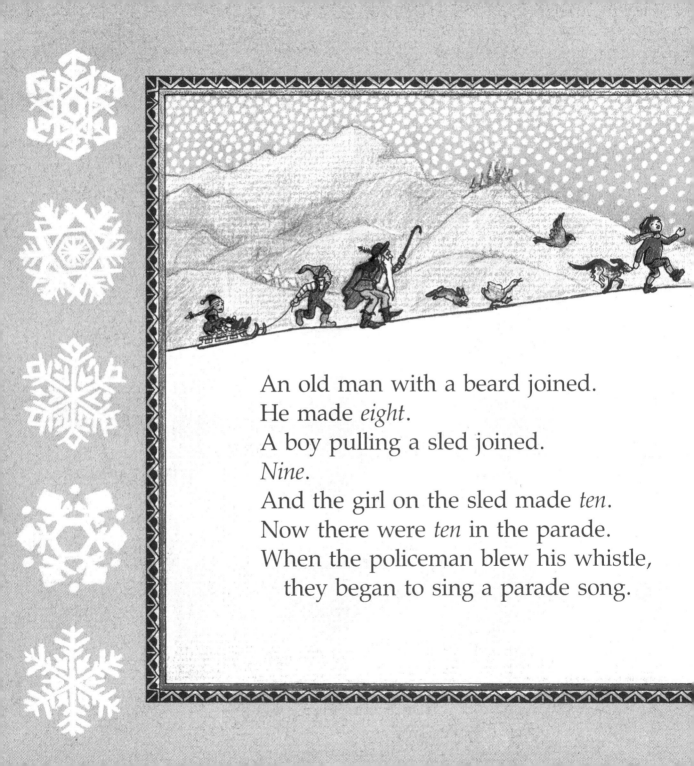

An old man with a beard joined.
He made *eight*.
A boy pulling a sled joined.
Nine.
And the girl on the sled made *ten*.
Now there were *ten* in the parade.
When the policeman blew his whistle,
    they began to sing a parade song.

Andrew sang the words.
The dog barked.
The duck quacked.
The pigeon cooed.
The rabbit chittered.
The horse neighed.
And the old man waved his cane
  in time to the music,
  while the boy and girl on the sled
  sang harmony.

Now others joined the parade.
Mothers with baby carriages.
Boys and girls on bicycles.
Folks in buggies.
People came out of their houses
    and even the squirrels came out
    of their holes in the trees
    to join the parade.

Ten. Twenty. Thirty. Forty. Fifty.
One Hundred. Five Hundred. More.

Soon you couldn't count them all,
   because there were just too many.

And Andrew Barclay said,
    "Now this is what I call a parade."